Jay G

John Gumbs

Published by John Gumbs
Publishing partner: Paragon Publishing, Rothersthorpe
First published 2019
© John Gumbs 2019, London

ISBN 978-1-78222-656-7

Book design, layout and production management by Into Print
www.intoprint.net
+44 (0)1604 832149

Contents

1

The Planting and Weeding of the Sugar Cane

WE WORKED IN what we call a gang of eight or ten men. We plant the sugar cane with a pick ax. The plant is already dropped into rows and we just go along and plant them into the ground. After some months, I heard the men complaining over their pay. I decided to do something about it the next time the overseer came up on his horse.

It was about lunch time when I approached him. He was sitting on his horse waiting for the lunch break to finish. I went up to him, he was surprised to see me so close to his horse.

"What do you want Jay G? Get to work, they're wasting time."

I said, "We'll go back to work according to the rule book, 12:30 pm."

"We will see about that," he said, and turned his horse rapidly so that the horse's left foot stamped on my right foot which was bare. The pain was excruciating. I fell over, grabbing my right foot with both hands. Some of the men came over quickly and carried me away to get first aid.

The overseer was a white man, tall with a thin straw hat on his head. Looking at him, one could see that he was fit. I knew he didn't like me, he tried his best to niggle me. He knew that I was clever more than the others in the group; he knew he could do whatever he liked with them, but when it came to me, he had problems. From the start I had been asking for more pay. He didn't like that. He had the way of making up all sorts of excuses, and to make us forget about ever asking again for higher pay.

My foot got healed rapidly. I was lucky that no bones were broken. My foot had sunk in the soft soil, at the same time the horse had stamped on it. In the yard around knocking off time, he was there giving his horse water. He was on the right side of the horse holding its reins. I was on the opposite side speaking to him over the horse's back.

"It is me you've got to deal with, and with no one else in my gang. I'm the one who will defend them."

"We don't like people like you on the estate," he said, patting the horse on its side.

"Of course you don't like me because I can read, I know the history of my people. I know how your people came here and killed off my ancestors. However, watch out for yourself, because you're not going to get rid of me that easy."

"Wait and see," he said, taking his horse away from the water.

In the town I was outside one of these drinking bars playing domino. When we play this game we make a lot of noise by slamming the pieces hard on the table. I got up from the board, stepped into the bar. The counter was long and smooth. I slammed a coin on the counter and called for four drinks. The barman turned around, took up the coin and served me. As I stepped out the bar, there were five white youngsters. As I went to sit down, one of them kicked the seat away. I lashed out at him with a right, but he was very quick. He gave me a kick in the groins which sent me down on my knees, then I felt a backhander, and I crashed to the ground. The other three guys who were playing dominos with me were lucky. The white youngsters only had it in for me, and I suspect they must have had orders from that overseer.

2

Arawaks, Caribs, Spaniards, French, Italian, English, Dutch

ON THE MONDAY morning in the yard, on the estate, I saw that overseer. I went over to him and said, "You had to get others to do your dirty work for you, but here I am, still in one piece."

He climbed up onto his horse, looked back at me, "For how long?" Then he rode away.

On this day the gang and I had this field plowed and hoed, and the plants lying in their rows, ready to be planted. We would come along with the pick ax, dig it in the ground to make a hole, then put the plant in, with the tip sticking out.

At the end of the day the field was finished and we moved to another. As we were knocking off, one of the men in the gang said to me, "That overseer, hates you, man. He doesn't see eye to eye with you."

I said to him, "Do you know why? They're the ones who killed off our ancestors, the Arawak. They took their land, and now they're making us work it for little or no money."

"What do you know about those people?" He questioned.

"The Europeans came down and took over the islands. They fought among themselves. The tribes who were originally on the islands were killed off. You want me to carry on?"

"Sure, brother! I'm listening," he said while some more men came close by.

"I read about the Arawak," I carried on, "how they were a peaceful people and hated war. Women or men could be their leaders. If there was trouble around them they would take all that they owned and went away. They enjoyed fishing and loved to eat fruits. Cassava was one of their main meal. Also star-apples, corn, cashews and guava. Their enemies were the Caribs who were cannibals.

The Arawak lived without clothes. The men do not work at home, they were hunters. While the women looked after the cassava plant, the men lie about in their hammocks. The Arawaks kept themselves in a cleaner state than those of the Europeans."

"So they are our ancestors? They were very peaceful. You have to tell me some more tomorrow, I really like the stories of the past especially if they are true."

"Tomorrow," I told him, "I will tell you about the Caribs." We then departed to our homes.

Out in my yard, I had three stones ready with the wood placed there. I fancied making some dumplings, peas and sweet potatoes. I had brought with me some fresh fish. As I knelt down on both knees, bending over low to the ground to blow wind into the fire, I felt the presence of someone near. I rose up.looked to my right, and there was that overseer. I said, "What you're doing here, get away from me or I'll sling you out my yard."

"I see you're having trouble with your fire, you need some help?"

"I dont need any help from you at all, we are nature people and we know how to make a fire burn."

"Nature people? Huh! Are you trying to fool me? Cant you see I'm above you and that you're my slave. Why don't you wake up and face reality."

"You would like that to be so, I'm not your slave. When I work, there are my bosses who are full of justice. With you, you don't like me and we'll never get on."

"Because you can read, you think you know it all. What are you planning to do? Make your gang break away from their work and their masters?"

"You know quite well that I'm not trying to do such a thing. All I want for my gang is that their pay for the work that they're doing is good. Is that asking too much?"

"Any time I see you're stepping out of line, I'll come down heavy on you. I have already spoken to the higher ones, and they know what they should do."

"You probably told them all lies. You live on lies, but I'm not like you. Now get out my yard and let me be!"

He left immediately and I carried on with my cooking. The sun wasn't far from setting and you could see the yellow-red glow across the sky. I sat down and had a nice tasty meal.

When I went in to work, my gang and I had to spread soda on the sugar cane plant. At the beginning of the field there were many crocus bags filled with soda for spreading at the roots of the young sugar cane. Each one of us took a row and started spreading the soda. It didn't take us long to finish this field. The next one we tackled was a large one. While we were halfway through the big field, a tractor with a cart loaded with soda came by. We unloaded it and it drove back to the yard. We took a break around 10:00 am and I got the chance to tell the gang some more about their ancestors.

"The Caribs," I began, "were a very war-like tribe. They were responsible for killing off the Arawak tribe along with the Europeans. They called themselves by the name "Kalinago." The Carribean sea is named after them. They moved about from island to island in the Lesser Antilles. They were called the Galibi. They did many raids among the Arawak, taking away their women. They like fishing and to make baskets. They were good at navigation, they used canoes.The Caribs hair was long and black, and loose. Sometimes they painted their skin with vegetable mixture. They use war clubs, bows and arrows. They were accused of being cannibals."

The whole gang was pleased with what they heard.

I said to them, "I'll tell you more later, about the Spaniards."

An hour before knocking off, I had to go and see the estate manager. Up in the yard, I had to climb a few stairs before I came to where the manager was housed.. I waited for a while, and then he asked me in. When I was seated, he asked if I wanted some lemonade. I said, "No thanks."

He poured himself a glass. "What's this I'm hearing," he finally said to me, "that you're having problems with my overseer.. You yourself is a very good gang leader. We need men like you."

I said to him, "We just can't get on, as simple as that."

"I'll have a good talk with my overseer. I hope things work out peacefully in the future."

I went out from the estate manager knowing that it won't happen the way he wanted it to be.

On Friday, we were standing in a queue waiting for our names to be called to get our pay. When all the gang had been paid, my name was called. I went to collect and found my pay was not right. There was nothing I could do at that moment. I just had to accept what had been given and wait until Monday to put in a complaint. Some of the shops that I had owed money have to wait until the next week. On Sunday I watched some International cricket. This relaxed me some, and kept me from going haywire.

Next Monday, up in the yard, I put in my complaint and they said they would look into it. The overseer came with the work we had to do for the day. It was high up in the mountains.

We had to weed a few fields that had already sprung up. About waist high they were. About three o'clock in the afternoon, I saw five horses coming up to the field where we were. When they arrived where we were, they dismounted, still with the reins in their hands. They surrounded me, knocked me to the ground, and the overseer with his whip started beating me. I cry out, but there was no help. After a while, they left, and the men in my gang came over, and comforted me. My back felt as if it was split in two, and the pain was unbearable. There were marks on both my hands, trying to stop the whip as it came down on me.

We came back in the yard on Friday after noon so that we could collect our pay. When I had mine, it was correct. They had listened to my complaint. There were many gangs in the yard all getting ready, after pay, to depart. I saw that overseer tying up his horse to a pole. He went around the back of a long house, and I followed him. He was just about to open his slash when I attacked him. I didn't think at that time whether it was right or wrong to do so, I just did it. He was very quick. I knew he was fit and could handle himself. I was not in the mood for backing out. Out of the corner of my eye, I saw some of the men from my gang looking at us.

His right hand quickly grabbed me around the neck and tugging me into him. With my left hand I found his belt and latched onto it, and I pulled. We both hit the ground and rolling around. With my right hand I gave him one right in the gut. His left hand was, trying hard to get to my face, but I didn't give him the chance. Then, I heard a shout from the gang, and I knew I had to get away from him, which I did. Neither one of us was hurt badly. It was only a scrap. His men came and took him away. There were big grins on the faces of the men in my gang.

Saturday night I went to the movie to watch a western with

some of the men in my gang.It was a great movie. Later, we went and had a few drinks at one of the bars.

It is the second Monday in March. The gang and I has to work in the yard clearing out the stables and feeding the horses. The area around the molasses tanks must be kept clean. Also the horses drinking place. We also had to take a tractor with a couple carts, go to the capitol by the wharf and pick up goods.

We were back out in the fields when the week had ended. I saw the overseer quite often as he went out and came into the yard. There were no incidents between that whole week I worked in the yard.

The time came for us to spread megasse through the fields. Every time we took a break, I would tell them about the history of the West Indies. One day we had a long break, I told them about Columbus. Some asked, "Was he Spanish or Italian?"

I answered; "He was Italian, and he always had this thing about sailing. He had lots of plans and ideas. He believed he could sail west and reach Asia. So he set out and ended up in what we call "the Americas."

"He made four journeys from Spain. With three ships in the beginning, the Nina, Pinta and Santa Maria, he set sail on his first journey. It was on the 3rd August 1492 that he started out. In October, he landed at San Salvador, the first time that he came in contact with native indians.

At the end of the work day, the gang heard from me many things about Christopher Columbus. I let them know that he was very powerful, so powerful was he that when Ferdinand and Isabella sent a governor to take over from him, he refused to hand over. He was wrapped up in chains and sent back to Spain.

Columbus, on his first trip, had left some men behind and went back to Spain, taking some captives with him and some gold. When he returned, he found them all murdered."

I promised the gang to tell them more.

There was a feast in the evening close to the bay. This feast goes back to the time of the Arawaks. There was a big iron pot in the middle of the area on three big stones. The fire was burning furiously. The family and friends of the couple were in a circle near the pot. Guests and others were in a circle behind them. He was there: that overseer.

I started to feel uneasy, I was getting ready to enjoy this feast. Now the presence of that overseer has given me bad feelings. The feast started off with some of the men and women dancing bare chested around the pot. After that the warriors did a mock fight. There were lots of food around, many different kinds of fruits, and cassava cakes.

When the feast was over, a few men from a gang I know told me that the overseer was in trouble. On his way out of the compound, he was kidnapped and taken to a grove of trees. What I heard didn't go down too well. Hurriedly, I made my way to the grove of trees, and saw the overseer tied to a tree. As soon as he saw me, he said: "You're in for it this time!"

I drew closer and said to him, "I had nothing to do with this. I do not bend that low!" Then I turned to those who had captured him, "Untie him. This is not my doing."

Two of them went and untied the ropes. When the overseer was free, he said, as he was going away, "You have done a foolish thing, and you shall surely pay for it."

The sugar cane plant was now very high, in a few months time it will be cut down. We were doing the last weed. I was deep in the middle of the field, with the gang out at the edges, when again, I was overtaken by the overseer and a couple other men. I tried to lift the hoe that I had been working with to defend myself but it was not possible,. the three men were upon me like a flash. I fell to the ground with my head half in the roots of the sugar cane. You can get cut quite easily from the stalk of the cane. I felt blood trickling down the side of my left face. The blows just kept on coming in. The overseer was also busy with his whip. In the distance I heard someone calling my name. "Jay G, where are you?"

I had enough breath to shout back, "Over here!"

Four of the gang who had been weeding the edges came rustling through. The overseer and his men disappeared through the thick sugar cane. When the men in my gang got to where I was they asked if I was okay. They helped me up from the ground and took me out to the edge of the field. After work when I got home, I visited the hospital which was only 100 meters from where I live. They looked at the bruises on my body, did some tests to make sure there were no broken bones.

The month of June was here and it was time for cutting the cane. Before that, the gang heard lots of history from me. I told them how Columbus later moved from San Salvador and went to Cuba. He found another island which he named after Spain, Hispaniola. At Hispaniola, the Santa Maria was crippled. Only the Nina and the Pinta could sail. There was a terrible storm in the Atlantic when they were sailing with the Nina and the Pinta. They were separated but managed to get to Palos on the same day.

I had a gang now of ten men. Each one had a machete to cut the cane. Our first field was one which had thirty rows. That meant each man had three rows to cut. The overseer came around to check. I had no problems with him at this time. He would be absolutely foolish to try to upset me with a machete in my hand. I would not have used it in case of trouble. I would have gone to him barehanded.

At lunch break, the men all sat around eating their fish and rice and listening to me telling them about the Spanish in the West Indies.

"Let me not disturb your meal," I told them, "but when the Spanish came to the West Indies they committed many atrocities. On their horses they had lances and spears, they began to commit murders and much painful cruelties. They would take the little children from their mothers, and smashed their heads against the cliffs. Some of them they threw in the rivers; others they would put immediately to the sword. 'Some' of the Lords and nobles they roasted over a grill.

The Spaniards had a law: if one Spaniard die, a hundred Indians would pay. Many of the native Indians fled to the mountains. An officer was given 300 Indians to work in the mines; at the end of three months, only 30 was alive. In three to four months more than 6,000 children died, their mothers and fathers had been sent to the mines. The Spanish said that they came to the West Indies to serve God and to get rich.

One of the men asked: "Are you making all this up? Did the Spanish really behaved that way?"

I said: "Man, I'm telling you what's written in history. I know they did a lot of horrible things to the peaceful Indians. The Dutch by the way, were teaching the Arawak children and they ended up speaking 'Patois,' a mixture of Arawak and Dutch.

You know the West Indies became a real battle field with the French along with the Caribs fighting against the British. All the large islands were under Spanish control. In 1508, they made a garrison in Puerto Rico; and Jamaica in 1509; Cuba in 1515. One time they transported 40,000 Arawak Indians to work in the mines of Hispaniola. The Caribs didn't give up, they made many attacks on the British. It later became too much for them and handed themselves over."

After lunch and my little history chat, we went back cutting the cane. Behind us we could see the cattle pulling the carts heavily along; and the men loading them with the cane. There were the water girls and boys with buckets of water upon their heads, some heading towards us, others going to the cattle carts. One of the gang had good luck, his row had finished abruptly in the middle of the field. When the day for working came to an end, we packed up and went home.

3

Constable Work

LOOKING THROUGH THE town's daily news I saw this notice asking for constables. I decided that it would not be a bad thing in trying to be a constable. Okay, it's a bit lower than a police officer but I still can give out summons and confiscate goods. I was thinking now, too, that if they take me on I would be well away from that overseer. I would still see my old fellow-workers; have a drink with them now and then.

I applied for the job of constable and they took me on. I got extra training while I was working. In our community, people who misbehave are told to report to the police station. If they fail to do so, after a week, they get a summons. I have given a couple of those out.

One day I accompanied a police officer about 500 meters from the station. We went to see this man to get him to come to the station and report himself. When we go to where he was, outside a bar, with both his legs spread out, we spoke softly to him. He hadn't seen me before so I had to introduce myself. I let him know that I was a constable.

"So you can't arrest me," he said, "and the policeman you have with you ain't enough."

"What do you mean?" I asked him.

He said, "I'm not coming, you'll have to get more policemen."

I tried to make him see sense, but he had a few already and was not in the mood to reason.

I said: "If that's the way you want it, I'll send for another policeman."

He burst out with a horrible laugh. "That's still not enough," he said.

He was a big stropping fella and I felt that the two of us, the policeman and myself could not handle him. Every time the policeman swung his baton, the man would just take it away from him and fling it away.

The policeman said to him, "You have really done it now, sir, abusing a policeman."

The man grinned. "Policeman! Look at you, you are only a kid. Go back to mammy!"

I said, "Please sir, would you come quietly?"

"I just told you, I'm not going anywhere."

We got word back to the station and a few more policemen were on their way, all with batons. I could have taken this guy single -handed, but that was really asking for trouble. He probably would have torn me to pieces, but who knows? Being big doesn't always make you the victor, it is an advantage. Something stopped me from going into him. I didn't like the way he talked to the young policeman. I stayed my hand and waited for help to come.

When they got where we were, they moved in quickly without waiting for us. The man, laid a few policemen on the ground so that they were hurt. We finally got the man to the station after some more policemen were sent making the total twelve.

The man was really beaten up with the batons and, at the station he was thrown in one of the cells. He was then looked over by a doctor who happened to be there at the time.

Later, I found myself at the courts with a case of someone who had got their goods taken away. They had failed to pay a sum of money.

About a month and a half, I was assisting some detectives

along with some policemen on a murder case. I was lucky to be on this one because it had something to do with the sugar cane fields where they suspect the killer was hanging out.

This killer had chopped up his wife, bagged her, and took her out in a boat to sea. There was a storm later that brought the bag and its remains to shore. The killer then went on the run and hadn't been caught as yet. When I had heard it all, I said to the two detectives, "You have to catch this man, he's sick. He needs to be put away from the community."

"We'll catch him," they told me, "with your help. He is lurching somewhere in one of those fields and you know the area very well."

"That's true!" I replied. "All the fields on the estate are named. Like the field high up in the mountain near to the ridge is called 'Crystal Ridge.' The one down to the main road where the left hand side has no houses, is called 'Low Shops.'

One of the detective said, "The cane is now very high, somehow we have to flush him out. The other, the dark-haired one said, "Once we know which field he's located in, we can move in row by row. What I find rather difficult is that the fields are so close to each other. He can just slip from one to the other."

I said: "We should have had some way of looking down on the field to spot where he was hiding."

The tall detective asked, "Which field do you think is the thickest around this time/?" "They're all thick and full of thrash," I told them. "We've already started cutting in one field, so he won't be definitely in that one."

The tall one asked, "What made you change over and become a constable?"

"It was always in me from childhood. And all those comic heroes fighting to defend the law."

"I see," he said. "Have you got any law-abiding people in your family? I mean someone who is or was in the forces."

"Not that I know of," I told him. "My family are law-abiding people."

"Tomorrow," he told me, "we'll chat again over this case and try to come up with some ideas"

I went away and found an ice stall where I got myself a cold mauby and a piece of cassava cake. There was a nice beautiful breeze with the sun pouring down.

I must say I like those two detectives, and I feel that being around them would work out well. I was thinking of an idea to cordon off each field and get men to walk through row by row. One of the detectives had the same idea, but he didn't broaden it out. I was thinking about the other estates that were nearby. It would be a disaster for us if the killer escaped to one of them.

I was in a very deep state of thinking when someone touched me. It was one of my old workers. He had the day off. He said to me, "Man, you're a constable now. Have you settled in, or do you want to come back and cut cane? I heard about that killer. What's happening, man?"

I said to him, "Glad to see you, but we haven't a clue where he is. Your guess is just as good as mine. I've settled in well, working with two brilliant detectives. We'll come up with something.!"

He said, "Catch you around, man! Good work you're doing."

"Thanks! Take care!"

The following day I met the two detectives in a room at the police station. We began to discuss the case.

One of the detectives, the tall one said to me, "We"ve had a report that someone saw a man who resembles who we are looking for. He was alone and walking through a path between two sugar cane fields, then he disappeared.

We hurriedly got out of the station, got to the field we were told about and set a cordon around it. This field wasn't a big one, it had about ten rows. So we had to set a man on each row and then walk through. The cane in their bunches were tall and fat with lots of thrash and stalk hanging in all different direction. No one can walk through a cane field without getting slight cuts from the stalks. For them not to get cut, they'll have to be protected.

I was on the fifth row, then the signal was given and we started off through the cane field. I had problems getting through because the cane in one root, in one row, sometimes hang over to the row above or that below.

From experience, I know after walking, how far I was from the middle and the end of the field. The man above me was still some paces ahead of me. The one below me had long gone. As I pushed forward, and came to a cluster of cane in my way, I stooped down to clear the hanging cane when I felt a whack across my back. As I turned around, I saw the shining machete coming towards me. I managed to kick out while I was on the ground, rolling away very quickly.

One of the strokes got stuck in a fat cane, by the joint, and that's when I made my move and landed him one with my right, at the same time trying to get his hand away from the handle of the machete. This guy was tough, he grabbed me, and sent me flying in the thrash and the root of an open bunch. he came at me, and I got hold of his shirt and pulled with all my might, he came tumbling down as I moved out his path. I was just about to give him a kick with my boots when someone behind me shouted, "No, Jay G, don't!"

I was furious, but I listened. It was one of the detectives with a few men with him. "That's not the man," he told me, "that we're are looking for. But you've bump into one that is wanted for sometime for armed robbery.

I said to him, still breathing heavily, "I know he wasn't our catch but I had to defend myself.

The policemen came and took the criminal away.

Standing on the tractor path between the two cane fields, both detective praised me for what I did. The short one said, "We would have been burying you, had you not defended yourself well. Good work!"

Just before the policemen's ball, the detectives and I came up with another plan.

4

Crystal Ridge

CRYSTAL RIDGE IS high above the estate. It is a ridge just above the last cane field. Many of the fields around Crystal Ridge were on a slope. The tractors and cattle with their carts could not venture there. The men and women had to bring the cane, once it was cut, onto level ground where it would then be packed in the carts.

Right on top of the ridge, in the middle part, were a few tall trees, and it was very easy from that position to see in the distance anything that moved.

It was now late July and the cane cutters were well into the fields and cutting them down. The rows in the fields around Crystal Ridge would stop in one place, and start again after a few meters. Just under the trees in the middle was an over hanging cliff. I knew this area well because we had to plant the fields and fertilize them. Now they were tall and thick, hard to get through.

These fields were a very long way from the estate. The tractors with their carts got there quickly, but the cattle and their carts took some time. The water girls and boys had to know exactly where Crystal ridge cane fields were. Some of them would get lost if they were new and had been given directions. You had to know where the fields were, and by names.

It took us quite a while to get the largest estate manager to agree to our plans. He had first to get in touch with his bosses and the high officials before he gave us permission to do what we planned.

At a couple of meetings I did see that overseer but nothing happened between us. He was there because he knew the whole estate, where everything was.

The plan the detectives and I had been to burn a few cane fields, especially those down by "Low shops", and "Long road," this one was on the way to the estate.

It was not a very good thing burning the fields. The stalk on the sugar cane is gotten rid of but there is much pollution in the atmosphere, and the people in the town do not agree with the plan of burning. You can smell it, its not nice; and the ash lands every where carried by the wind. There's a very high temperature when the field is burning, but this cools down very quickly. The cane cutters have to move in immediately for if the field is left too long, the sugar cane become dry and people can use it for fire wood.

Some estates like to burn their fields, but this large estate we were dealing with prefer to have their sugar cane fields in a normal state. They have only given permission because of this murder case.

The detectives arranged for some policemen to hang out by the tall trees at Crystal ridge, and to keep a good look out. Down at Low shops we examined a field that was very close to the houses. Only a small track separated them. This cane field had a lot of thrash more than some of the others. It was really thick inside.

I was thinking, would the killer dare to be so cheeky as to hold up in there? At night time it would be for him to come out, get what he needed, and get back in. No. He wouldn't risk that. Some killers are very clever, and I think he is one of those clever ones.

The detectives and I along with a few policemen got ourselves ready to set fire to "Low shops."

The field was cordoned off with policemen, and then it was set on fire. It wasn't long before the whole field was ablaze. The fire was red and yellow, with billows of black smoke.

After a while it was all over. All the thrash and stalk were burnt away just leaving the cane either standing or sloping. Many people had come out to watch the burning, many school children too. That same afternoon, rain poured down and cooled the field. The next morning early, the cutters were in. There was no sign of anyone holding up in that field. No one had broken through the cordon.

Nothing much happened after the burning of Low shops. The policemen's ball was here, and it turned out to be a very big party. There were steel bands playing, stalls were set all around the compound. It was a very hot day so the men wore shirts and trousers. It went down well. There were lots of food, fruits of all sort. This policemen's ball was also for raising money for charity.

Everyone were enjoying themselves at the policemen's ball. I wasn't far away from the double gates to the compound. I was just on the left. The compound was pretty big and went way back with high walls. On top of these walls people would look down into the compound even when the young policemen were training. Sometimes the children climb up into trees to get a look down into the compound. I was talking to a young recruit when I happen to look up onto my right and saw a strange figure.

I stood there for a while pretending that I hadn't seen anything. then with a burst of speed, I left the young policeman and moved to the right where the double gates were. Out of the gates, I turned quickly to my left, a few meters up the road, then left into the trees and where the top of the compond walls were.

The strange man wasn't there. I looked to my right and saw this person running through a yard with a stilted house on the right. He ran out through an open gate and across the main road and up a lane leading to where men were packing sugar cane on the rail trailers. He went quickly to the field that was just behind the sugar cane packers. He didn't stop to look back. He knew that I was close behind him.

Inside the sugar cane field I could hear him tumbling through. I still kept the pace up. He managed to get out of the field just ahead of me. He went straight through the next one directly opposite. I stood on the track between the two sugar cane fields, trying to catch my breath. Out of the corner of my eye I saw a group of men coming along the track from the left. It was detective Brown, the tall one and detective Sampson, the short one, with some policemen. When they got to where I was Detective Brown said, "You almost got him!"

"The man is like a mongoose, he's as quick as ever. I think he's also an expert in those sugar cane fields." I told him.

Detective Sampson said: "Well spotted. We'll take him yet.

Packers field was just above where the packers were packing the sugar cane on rail wagons to be taken by train to the sugar-mill factory.

We left the area and went back to the station. There we had a drink and talked about what had happened.. I left the station and went to my home.

At about 02:00 am the next morning, a couple of policemen came to me. I had to report immediately to the station. Detective Brown and Sampson were waiting for me. They explained to me why they had called me. They told me the whole story, then we were off.

A boat had been seen down by the treasury house, out upon the sea, with a lone figure in it. When we got to the treasure house which was not that big, Detective Brown said: "If he's our man, he's really playing us for fools."

On our right the small beach ended with lots of rocks and a high hill. On top of that hill was a small house. The man in the boat must have seen us even though it was a little dark. He started rowing fast. "If he gets behind the rocks and the hill, we've no chance of grabbing him, if he's our man," detective Sampson said. "Over the hill, the sugar cane fields are very close to the sea just behind a row of trees."

'I said, "I know, and I'm now thinking, if he gets there before us, he can slip into the fields."

We got some policemen to go round the hill which took some time. A couple others were trying to cross the rocks on the right just below the hill, but it was very hazardous. Detective Brown, Sampson and myself started to walk up the track leading up to the top. It was steep. When we finally got to the top, we looked down to the shoreline and saw the little fish boat heading towards the shore.

Policemen were already in boats that were there, but not belonging to them, and chasing him. He had already gotten a good start on them.I noticed on the other side of the hill directly in front of us were trees on a deep slope down to the shore. I had to take the chance by running down very quickly, hoping that I do not knock myself against any of those big trees.

There was also a track to be seen. The detectives thought it was a bit dangerous, but was worth a try. I went down the hill sort of half running and holding back a little, keeping my eyes open, for it was still dark. the man in the boat got to the shore as I got to the bottom of the hill. He came close to the volcanic sandy beach, left the boat and was heading across the sand to get to the line of trees, and then to the fields just behind. I began to run across the sand seeing the darkened figure in front of me. This was really hard work, it was tough, taking energy out of me. This sand wasn't white and soft--it was pretty hard, and it took quite a lot out of me, with every step I took. The figure wasn't far from me when I made the leap and caught his right foot. he had a bag in his right hand and he lashed out with it. I was on the ground stretched out still holding on, he pulled away, only dragging me with him. I wanted to topple him over, but he was strong and would not let me do so.

If I only could get my left hand up, I could have the chance of a double grab, but it wasn't going to be so, I was lying on the sand awkwardly, I could feel pain coming through my body from the grating of the coarse sand.

If those policemen who went around the right side of the hill were here, things would have worked out differently, but as it is, I have to think of something quickly. I did. I don't know where the energy came from but I held on to his right leg, then I swung with both feet to the left and brought him down. He made a groan, grovelling in the sand, wriggling forward.

I immediately let his foot go, crawled behind him and gave him a right elbow in his back, then with both my hands, I grabbed his head, and started pulling backwards..

I don't know how he did it but he twisted himself out of my grip, started throwing sand in my face, which was lethal; he scrambled away in the dark of the trees and in the nearby sugar cane field. This angered me so much that I started banging on the dark sand with both hands, still in the kneeling position.

On my right on the hill side coming down to where I was, the policemen with searchlights.

I said to them: "I damn near had him."

One of them said, "Another time will come, sir!"

Detective Brown and Sampson who were watching from

the top of the hill met us as we came into view from the track on their left hand side.

The policemen who had taken the boats with oars to chase the man took the boats back. The other policemen could not get around the rocks.

Sampson said, "We thought you had him. He's a clever one. He got away. He's lucky, if we were closer or even on the beach itself, he would have been behind bars. He makes our task even harder."

I was still in an angry state. "We'll get the bastard. We'll get him."

It was now coming up to around 06:00 am when we knocked off. It wasn't worth it to go to bed. I took the town's daily news and looked through it.

This day, I gave out a few summonses and heard nothing but cursing and bad language coming from those who I gave the summons to.

Back from the court house, I popped into a soft drink place, got myself a bottle of ginger beer and a cassava cake. I like my cassava cake, nice and healthy. I started to think about how I went down that dangerous slope down to the volcanic beach. The two detectives who were with me couldn't do anything because they were on top the hill. I had the killer there in my grasp, and he got away. Next time I'll make sure he gets locked away.

5

Eight Trees

A TIP OFF came in that our man had been seen by the "Eight Trees" and the old broken down houses. We immediately got ourselves there. We were about 500 meters away surveying the area. Directly in front of us were eight trees and some broken down houses. Behind them was the beginning of the sugar cane field.

We sent a number of polcemen to the left up the track, while we sent some more to the right. They were to up and surround the sugar cane field that was above the eight trees.

A few of the houses were on walled bases. They were supported by wooden stillts.

Detective Brown said: "We have to play this very carefully. If we rush in too quickly, it may all go wrong. As soon as he sees us move, he has the cane field behind him. Our policemen behind and at the sides of the field could apprehend him should he take that route."

I said, "He could go into the field and try to escape into another. The cordon has to be very tight so that he cannot slip through."

It was coming up for midday, the sun was pitching down from above. There was a cool breeze. The detectives and I and the policemen we had with us moved up slowly. We spotted him, he was behind one of the eight trees.

These eight trees were in a row, a few meters apart. Their branches hang onto each other. We were now in a long line and very close, so that he had no chance to slip through us. We sent word to those at the back of the field and to the side for those policemen to be vigilant and don't let him get through.

The sugar cane field directly behind the eight trees in a line, was named after them. On its left there was another field. In fact, there were many fields close to each other. It made it much harder to trap him should he slip through the cordon. Detective Brown and Sampson received strong words from their Commissioner. He wanted them to speed things up, and get this killer where he belong.

We had the idea that he was held up in one of the broken down houses but that wasn't so. From our position we saw movement behind one of the eight trees.

At 13:30 pm Detective Brown gave the order to move in. We did so. We got to the broken houses, to the eight trees and there was no one there. He must have slipped through "Eight Trees" before we had time to set up the cordon. I was thinking fast now. How could he have slipped away when we saw movement at one of the trees, and we had already sent the policemen to the side and at the back. I said to Sampson, who was nearby, "This is the time when we should have had tracker dogs. He would have been in dead trouble."

"These people don't work with tracker dogs," Sampson told me.

"Why is that?" I asked him.

"I don't know what it is, but they have never given us tracker dogs. We can have any amount of policemen as we want, but tracker dogs, no chance."

We moved up to the border of the cane field to where detective Brown was with a few policmen beside him. "He's in there," he said, pointing to 'Eight Trees'. The rows in the field were diagonal with the shortest one not far from us. Detective Brown still couldn't understand how he got away.

He was also deciding whether to set 'Eight Trees' alight. "What do you think?" He asked me.

I said, "If we knew for sure that he would stay inside there, then it's worth the gamble. But I personally don't think he would risk that."

"Okay!" Brown said, "Get the policemen down here. There were quite a lot of policemen. They gathered around us, and detective Brown gave them a lecture. When that was finished we all went back to the station.

Not one of us had thought about checking the eight trees that stood in a line. It didn't come into our heads because we knew no killer of his caliber would have taken the risk of hiding in the trees. The trees were tall and packed with branches. It was hard to see through to the top. We had checked all the broken houses and the surrounding area, and we found nothing.

Back at the station while all the policemen were out in the compound and having a fresh drink, detective Brown took Sampson and myself upstairs in a room. He said to us, "We should have our man by the end of the week."

I said: "How do you work that one out? What if he decide to stay low. We won't know where he is. There are many cane fields on the estate, and what if he moves across to another, we've lost him then."

He said, "We're going to go back to "Eight Trees," and we're the ones who will stay low. I've got the hunch, he'll come back there because it was an easy escape for him."

"And if he didn't come back?" I asked detective Brown, "What then?"

"What about the next village?" Sampson said. "There's not many of our policemen there. If he's smart, he'll want to go there."

"No, I don't think he'll do that,"I said, "he'll want to stay around on the big estate. He knows it well. He wouldn't risk going somewhere else."

Detective Brown said, Crystal Ridge was too high up in the mountain. We've wasted a lot of time going there."

I said: "That's true!"

Detective Brown said, "We'll have a big exercise. We'll pick an area where there's four sugar cane fields close to each other, only the track between them. We'll surround them but staying hidden in the first rows. That way, we could look onto the path and to the next cane field. Our dress will be the same color as the thrash in the field."

Detective Sampson said, "That is very clever, Sir, brilliant!"

I said, "I find it a very good plan, Sir. As soon as he comes out of one, planning to enter the other, we grab him. He's not in any way suppose to see us."

We went ahead with the plan, and the following day very early we set the policmen in the field next to "Eight Trees." "Eight Trees" is to have no policemen there., detective Brown told us. "This operation calls for fit policemen, they'll have to follow him through the field without giving up."

"But Sir," I said. "He's an expert going through those fields. It would be a miracle if our policemen could keep up with him."

"We'll see," Brown said, and we left the station after he told all the policemen in the compound about the plan.

The whole company of us were at the back of "Eight Trees" spread out along the second row from the tractor path which ran through both "Eight Trees" and the one directly opposite which was called "Pancake," the fact that it was very flat. Sampson was just on my right, with detective Brown on my left. Sampson was looking through his binoculars over into "Pancake." He thought he saw something moving, but he wasn't sure.

If anyone was walking along the track they would not have seen us, we were lying low and hidden.

Suddenly, there was our man, he came out of "Pancake, stood beside a bunch of sugar cane that were spreading mostly to the ground, he was looking up and down making sure the way was clear.

Sampson was gone. Leaving "Eight Trees, he rushed towards "Pancake, and towards our man. I think he saw Sampson first, turned around and headed back inside "Pancake."

Detective Brown shouted, "Sampson, what the hell are you doing?" Sampson didn't listen, at this moment, he didn't care. He saw his man and he wanted him. Rushing through a full grown cane field is not an easy task, especially if you're chasing someone.

Detective Brown directed the policemen what to do. They must get around quickly and cordon off the back and both sides of "Pancake." He and another group will stake out where they now were.. I was praying for Sampson to grab his man, knowing myself that it wasn't an easy thing to do. Sampson kept up the pace with the killer who was heading in one direction. The killer had nothing sharp on him to defend himself. Just as he, the killer, got to the end of "Pancake" he found himself in trouble. "Pancake" levelled out, while the beginning of the next field was on a rise. Sampson made a leap toward his man just as both of them got out of the field. They both went down but there was nothing the killer could do. There were too many policemen waiting there and they came in immediately, using their batons and handcuffed their man. Detective Brown congratulated Sampson, but told him off for moving before orders were given.

6

Sorrell Ground

IF ONE WALKS THROUGH the main door of the police station, in our place, directly in front of them are the cells with only a bench inside. On the left at the end of the cells are stairs leading to the next floor. On the right, not far from the main door is a desk with a policeman seated behind it. Just next to him, on his left side is a door leading out to the compound.

At this station there were six policemen doing shift during the night hours. Five upstairs and one at the desk below.

The young policeman went over to the cell to give the killer a drink. The bunch of keys hanging on his right hip attached to his belt, he also had a blue land yarrd around his right arm with a whistle at the end of it. He had his baton with him.

At 10:00 pm, a big man came through the door, took hold of the young poiceman and warned him not to cry out, or he'll break his neck. Waiting outside was another man in an old jeep with the engine running. From upstairs, it is easy to see clearly down in the street. The off duty policemen were busy playing cards.

A van had already been ordered to come to the station to transport the killer to the capital the following morning. The big man held the young policeman fast as he got the keys from his side. The keys were all marked and it was easy for the big man to take the one he wanted. He placed the key in the iron lock, turn, and the door opened. The killer came out and as the big man got to the main door still holding the young policeman, some women who had seen what was going on screamed so loud that the policemen upstairs heard the noise. They went to the window to investigate and saw the jeep racing away.

They immediately ran down the stairs and saw the cell door open, and the young policeman on the floor at the door holding his arm in pain. One of the policeman from upstairs went and took statements from the onlookers on the other side of the road. Another policeman took a bicycle and peddled away to inform detective Brown what had happened.

I heard the news when I was walking away after the cinema was closed. people were talking about a break in at the police station, and how a young policeman was beaten up. When I got to the station it was around 23:30 pm.

Detective Brown and Sampson were already upstairs in the room when I walked in. "We are back at the beginning," detective Brown said. "And we're in deep trouble with the commissioner."

I asked: "Am I included?"

Brown said, "You know why you're with us. Your help is very valuable. Wish we had more constables like you."

I said, "Thanks for the compliment. Any new plans?"

He shook his head. "There's now three of them we have to deal with. That makes our task even harder. I'm thinking now, where do we start. Let's gather all the information from the young policeman who was on duty when it all started; and also from the one who took statements from the women."

Sampson said, "Seeing now that there's three of them, he probably would abandon the cane fields. So we could be looking for them holding up somewhere in a house."

"I was thinking in that line as well, but it is quite possible that they could still use the cane fields," I said.

Brown said, "Now we have to be on our toes. We can't afford to slip up this time. We should have taken him straight away to the capital prison. We thought it was safe here for a one night stay. How wrong we were!."

"I'll keep my ears open for any news," I told him. "I have to be at the court house for a few cases."

Sugar cane fields bordered the small main road going to Sorrell Ground. Now and then you'll see some trees with bread fruits hanging on them, small coconut trees at the side. The first couple of meters was straight road, then it started to bend up and down, the the last kilometer straight into Sorrell Ground. There was a small estate way down close to the bay on the left -hand side.

Sorrell Ground was about 5 or 6 kilometers away. It had a few houses with the street going through it lined with telegraph poles and tall trees. Just on the left about 500 meters was a track leading down the bay. About the same distance along the road was another. The people living in Sorrell were very friendly and hospitable, you really hear of any trouble there.

In our community we always fight the lawbreaker without guns. There are special groups of policemen who use guns against those more terrible criminals who do smuggling between the islands.

The lawbreaker will always come against the police defending himself either with a knife or a machete, but never with a gun. Our policemen in the street only has a baton and a whistle. The lawbreaker gets captured, he gets clobbered with a policeman's baton.

Sorrell Ground is surrounded by cane fields around its back while the sea is at the front.

The court cases finished, I was taken to Sorrell Ground. I have never seen so many policemen in one area like this before. There was an open field just on the left before we enter Sorrell Ground. Detective Brown and Sampson were there just like they told me they would be. They asked me how the court cases went. I told them one got a week's jail, while the others had to pay a fine.

I said to detective Brown, "You're really going to flush them out this time!"

He said: "If we don't find them in Sorrell Ground it would mean that they're inside one of the cane fields, but they cannot stay there forever."

Sampson said: "Soon after a few months, the young shoots will be pooping out. We'll be able to see clearly then!"

Brown said, "We'll have them in prison before the new shoots come out. I have enough policemen to go in field by field. I mean business this time."

A policeman came up to Brown and said, "Sir, everything is ready. Shall we proceed through the first field?"

"Yes, go ahead, well done!" Brown told him.

He looked at me and said,"The whole back of Sorrell is cordon off. There is no way of them escaping to the sugar cane fields."

"I can see that!" I said to him. "What about the houses?"

"We'll check them one by one, starting with the first one here on the left." He pointed to it.

We started checking the village of Sorrell Ground. In some bushes at the back, just in front of the sugar cane field, we found some rum distilling equipment lying abandoned. We came to a house with a latch on the door and a stick in it. There was no one around. Some policemen stayed by watching the house.

We went up a road to our right for about a thousand meters, and then there on our right was a brick house with an old jeep before it. The young policeman at the station did not get to see the jeep but the women who saw what had happened, gave the description of this same jeep. They did not give the license number. Policemen surrounded the house, detective Brown went up to the door and knock on it. An old woman came to the door and spoke with detective Brown. The old woman said that jeep had been there for some months now, and had never left where it was. The jeep belonged to her son who was working in the capital. Detective Brown got all the information, and a message was quickly sent to the capital.

Sorrell Ground is not that far away from an island nearby. This island is about 10 kilometers away. Criminals normally go there by boat during the early hours of the night. They come back loaded with rum and cigarettes and other goods, only sometimes to find themselves in trouble with the special police.

After detective Brown dismissed the police, he, Sampson and myself stayed behind a little longer. The policemen had done their job. They had been through Sorrell Ground and found nothing. They drove back in trucks that were there.

Detective Brown, Sampson and I were down at the sea front. We had walked down a track and came to a small beach. On the right of us were some rocks sticking out the ground for about five meters. And a sandy stretch. The trees lining that stretch of beach hang down low. It was hard to see underneath them.

"What now?" I asked Brown, who was looking out to sea.

He turned to me and said, "We have to wait. Keep our eyes alert."

No sooner had he said that when a big man was pushing a boat down to the shore. Everyone of us started running in that direction. Sampson stumbled on the rocks that jotted out. Detective Brown was just in front of me. The small boat reached the shore line, the man hopped in, and as he did so detective Brown managed to grasp the boat hanging loosely in the water. The two oars hadn't been hooked up yet, they were lying in the middle of the boat. There was a small suitcase which the man grabbed and was using it as a hammer against the hands of detective Brown. The boat was hopping up and down with the waves, at the same time, out and down with the current. Detective Brown was still hanging on. He stayed like that for a while. I wasn't far from them, but they kept shifting away.

I leap into the water and found the going really hard. Detective Brown still in the water was trying to get a better grip. So that he could heave himself up and over. The small boat was now some distance out. And way down from where it started.

I've heard all those stories about the sharks. What do I care? I had no fear. I was doing my duty and no shark was going to put me off. I am now deep in the water trying to help my buddy; and to hell with the sharks. These waters were deadly. They were shark infested waters. It was very dangerous for Brown if he kept his body in the water much longer. A shark could come along and tear his body to shreds.

Sampson after he had picked himself up, sent a message back. As for me I had to give up. I wasn't achieving anything. I was swimming my guts out, and the boat was well away from me. I got back to the shore soaking wet and joined Sampson, we both looking in the direction of the boat. The man threw the case down and grabbed the oars and placed them in their metal frames. He started rowing. This gave detective Brown the chance to tumble in at the side. The man left the oars, came over and tackled Brown. Both of them now in the middle of the boat trying to overpower each other. From the message Sampson had sent, a police speed boat was on its way.

Sampson and I were now hoping that detective Brown would come out on top without getting too seriously hurt. The small boat was now too far away from us to see clearly what was taking place. We could still see the tall figure of dtective Brown but had no idea what was going on.

On our left, we saw the police speed boat going down to the small boat. It reached where they were in a few minutes. The speed boat had six policemen on board. The small boat was attached to the speed boat, after detective Brown and the other man had been taken on it.

They got back to where Sampson and I were, they came in close enough to let us know that the big man wasn't our man. He was just a smuggler. He always went down to the island to get cheap stuff.

Detective Brown I saw had some bruises on his face, and both his hands were plastered. We told that we would make our way back to the station. The speed boat left still with the small boat behind it. They had confiscatred it. The big man will be taken to the capital prison.

At the station, detective Brown filled us in with all that took place on the small boat. A van from the capital was already outside to transport the man away. His face was a bit swollen.

Detective Brown told us that at one time, the man had him against the side and was trying to heave him overboard. He said he held on with his right hand on the oar that was just beside him, and manaaged to get the man away. Many times they tumbled to the back and to the front; and at one time he thought the boat was going to turn over but it stayed upright.

After detective Brown was patched up properly, we went upstairs in the station to our usual room fo a chat.

I said: "I'm glad you're back in one piece. You were in a very dangerous position, Sir."

"I know," Brown said. "But we of the law are only interested in getting the culprit, and we have three of them still out there.. The driver of the jeep whoever he is, has got himself into trouble by being an accomplice. The big man who assaulted the young policeman is deep in trouble. We have the killer himself. All three have to be brought to justice. The young policeman saw this one we brought in and said that he wasn't the one. Our community is good at giving us tips everytime they see anything."

Sampson said, "Just trust me to slip at the moment when I should have been there in the heat of it!"

I said: "Thank your lucky stars. What if you had reach him first inside that boat. I think detective Brown did well. Not many men would have known how to handle the situation. First, it call for bravery and not having no fear. Some, I suppose would have given up, and let the man get away. But our Sir has done a pretty good job."

"Thank you, Jay G," detective Brown said.

"Sampson, you hear that? Detective Brown mention me by name."

"Now what you're getting at Jay G? I always knew your name."

"How's your hand Sir," I asked. "The way that man was banging that suitcase down upon your hands was terrible. I could see it was only a small case."

"If it hadn't been for the boat dipping now and then into the water, I would have had no hands to work with. Anyway, let's get down to some plans and ideas of catching those criminals." Brown told us.

"Any ideas? We've been through Sorrell Ground with a tooth pick and found nothing." I remarked.

Sampson said: "He could still be on the big estate in one of its cane fields. It is possible that he could still be on his own, but getting help from the other two."

Detective Brown said, "There's three of them, soon they'll make a slip up, and we'll move in."

"' I don't think it's going to be that easy, Sir. Some of those criminals are very clever. They like to harass us. They get pleasure in doing so." I said.

We thrashed out a few more ideas, then detective Brown said I could go away and if anything come up, they'll let me know.

The next day I was at the ice stand getting a crush ice with colouring over it. "Hello there!" It was Daphne, a school friend.

I said, "Hi! How are you doing?

"Fine," she said. "I see you have moved into the big time. From cutting cane to a detective."

"I'm only a constable," I told her.

"Given out any summonses lately? Have you got one for me?"

"Not really! I'm working alongside two detectives on the case of that killer who killed his wife."

"You haven't caught him yet? She asked. "The sooner the better."

"How's your love life," I asked her. "Not married yet? No kids?"

"I'm waiting around," she told me, "for somebody like you."

"That could be a long wait," I told her. "I'm so busy with my work."

"One day, you'll have to make up your mind." She told me..

"I know," I said. "I'm always thinking about it. For now, it'll have to wait."

"Good luck," she said, and went away.

"Thanks!"

I had to give out some summonses on the Friday and I found myself up in the yard of the big estate where that overseer worked. The groups were all there waiting for their pay. I gave out the summonses and was planning to leave when a few of my gang said: "You haven't told us what happened to the Caribs who were fighting for their island St.Vincent. I said, "I totally forgot, glad you remind me, and I was so busy on this murder case that I wasn't thinking about history any more."

"How you do with that murder case, anyway?" They wanted to know.

i said, "Things are tightening up, we came close a few times but we'll get there. Okay, I'll tell you quickly what took place at St. Vincent."

"While the Caribs were living on the island the French came and took it over, then later, the British. But for some unknown reason the Caribs and the British didn't get on. The first war between them ended with no one winning. The year was in 1773. There was peace between them until 1795. The French had control from 1779 to 1783. It went back to Britain by the Treaty of Versailles. The Carib chiefs were planning to attack the British in the year 1795. The two Carib chiefs wasn't planning for another treaty and fighting started.

One of the men said: "You mean the Caribs took on the British?"

I said , "Yes, man, that's what they did. They were good fighters. They decided it was worth it to fight for their home land.

The Caribs split up and started giving the British a hard time. At one time the British found themselves being attacked from the front and the rear. The two Carib chiefs were Joseph Chatoyer and Duvalle They were brothers. The black Caribs were known as the Garifunas. The original inhabitants of St. Vincent were the Ciboneys and Arawaks. They were replaced by the Caribs. The black Caribs were a mixture of African and Caribs. There were red Caribs and yellow Caribs. The red Caribs fought with Chatoyer. Some of the Caribs fought along side the British. There were French fighters mostly africans. Chatoyer's father was Legotte. Chatoyer had a daughter named Gulisi. He had sons as well.

The chief Duvalle and his men captured the post at Dorsetshire Hill. They celebrated, took down the union jack and set the flag of the French Republic in its place.

There are many stories of what happened between the British and the Caribs on Dorsetshire Hill. One story says that three English young soldiers were captured while the Caribs were on their way to Dorsetshire Hill. Joseph Chatoyer was in a rage when he got there. He hacked the three young soldiers to pieces. Another story said that the British forces killed Chatoyer; and yet another said that he challenged one of the British officers to a duel because there was a legend that he couldn't be killed by mortal hands. The British officer killed him, and it is said that the British officer died later from many wounds he got from Chatoyer.

There was more fighting, advancing and retreating, and more ships arriving, The Caribs were still there along with the French harassing the British. It was around 26th October 1796 that 5,080 Caribs surrendered. They were sent to Honduras away from their homeland. Duvalle and young Chatoyer were the last to give themselves up."

"Man, that is some history!" One of the men said, "very interesting!" I had to leave my old group and get back to the station. I hadn't seen the overseer at all. I left the yard and my old group behind me.

A woman who had been coming in from the mountain with brush-wood on her head, her donkey before her laden with things from the trees and the ground, saw a man acting strangely. He came out of "Half Mile" and as he saw her, he went back in.

As soon as the report came in, detective Brown wasted no time, he had all the police transported in trucks and up to "Half Mile." He immediately set a cordon around the top, bottom and the right side. The left side was very dangerous. It went down into a grassy steep valley. Police men were set on that side and was told to be careful.

It was Saturday, normally a time for relaxing and waiting for the Monday to appear. But when you're on a murder case, you can never really relax. Any minute there could always be something. Sometimes it brings a lot of drinking disorder where some men are put in the cell for the night.

We stood on the right side of "Half Mile" on the tractor track. I said to detective Brown,"What do you think, he's in there or has immediately taken to another field.?"

"It's hard to say," detective Brown answered. "Half Mile has only fifteen rows, but is rather thick and thrashy. I'll get some men to go in row by row."

I said, "I'll go in as well."

Sampson said: "Look out for yourself."

"I will." I said, and went through the field along with the men. It didn't take us long to get on the left hand side, standing at the top and looking down into the valley. There were mango trees, as we could see, lining a path down at the bottom. Coconut trees hang all over the place. While the men were looking down in the valley with their binoculars, one of them thought he saw someone moved from behind a mango tree. I wasn't going to wait if the sighting was true or not.

A coconut tree that was close by had some dry branches beneath it. I got one of them, broke off the stem, got on it and rode down on the green grass. I knew it was highly dangerous. One could end up breaking parts of the body, if one didn't steer out of trouble.

In the middle of the hill the coconut branch picked up speed and went down like a bullet. I saw the person climbing like mad on the other side. I had a feeling that it was our man. At the top was a sugar cane field lining the edge with lots of green foliage alongside. Looking over at the figure quickly, I forgot all about my journey downwards. The coconut branch that I was on ran straight to the bottom and into a mango tree. I was sent flying head over heels. I was lucky. I laid there for a while in pain. Nothing was broken. When I looked up on the hill, there was no one. The police men at the top behind me shouted down and asked if I was okay. I told them not to worry.I walked away saying: "Damn! Damn! Damn!"

Back at the station I had a soft drink. Sampson said," You're lucky to be in one piece. That's a very dangerous thing that you did. I remember as kids, some of us used to do that, and bumped into trees often. We'd end up with hurting all over."

"How do you think I'm feeling?" I said. "Full of pain still. I was born lucky."

Brown said, "Was that our man. Did you get a good look?"

"I'm not so sure. When he was climbing up the other side, it was hard to tell among all the trees on the hill. If it wasn't our man, why would he run away?" I explained.

Sampson said, "Criminals are always on the run. If he wasn't our man, then he must be a criminal."

Saturday afternoon late, we knocked off.

I was thinking, I could go to the movie for two hours. It looked like a good movie from the poster. I decided to go and look at it.

The town is always packed on a Friday and Saturday night, more so on Saturday night. People hanging around with trays of fruits, fried fish, peanuts, home made soup, and lots of cassava cakes. After the movie had ended, I walked around for an hour looking at the shops and all the stalls that were set outside at the side of the street. Then I headed for home. I live not very far from the station. Just a quick bicycle ride.

7

Gulley Bay Road

A FEW VILLAGES away was "Gulley Bay Road." It was so named because the road ran next to the sea; and on the left-hand side was a deep gulley about 600 meters in with cane fields on the top. On both sides of the gulley were all sort of trees. In the village itself, the road took a sharp right turn and then straightened out for a while, and then sharply turned to the right and then up through thick forest.

At the bend the sea came close touching the wall. It was very deep in that corner.

Trucks with policemen were already making their way to Gulley Bay Road. A jeep had been seen going into a garage, and not far away was the gulley.

There were stories about the gulley. Some say it was haunted. Others said that it was the place where men went to make deals with the unknown. Whatever the stories were, whether true or not, the gulley looked rather mysterious, thick with trees, dark and unappealing. There were canefields hanging over the border at the top.

We got there in good time. Detective Brown surrounded the place, but before he did so, the man had already left the house, and ran through a track on his left and to the gulley. There was a spacious place in front of the house.

Detective Brown and the police went up to the garage. It was locked. They broke it open. There was the jeep, the same one that had transported the killer away from the police station back in the town. Policemen had already found a way around the back, and was now at the top of the gulley. Detective Brown, Sampson and myself along with other policemen went down into the gulley. There was water running down the middle; and it went under the road and gushed out into the sea.

At the end of the gulley there was a small cave. We got our searchlights and switched them on. There were rats and small insects everywhere. About a hundred meters in the cave it splits into a fork. Detective Sampson and I with a few policemen went to the left while detective Brown with other policemen went to the right. We followed the left side until we couldn't stand anymore. We had to bend down. A few more meters and the cave came to an end. We got back to where we had started only to find that detective Brown had captured the man who owned the jeep. After his house was thoroughly checked, he was put in a police van and taken straight to the capital prison. The next day we went to the capital to have a chat with him. We gathered quite a lot of information from him. The big man who had come to the station and let the killer out was his brother. The owner of the jeep didn't know where he lived. As for the killer, he had no permanent place, the owner of the jeep said to us. It was already obvious to us that the killer was moving from place to place. The cane fields were his hide outs.

Back in our own town, two days later, I was on my bike riding along the road. I came to the the senior boys and girls school which had three entrances. A big massive double gate on the left side, a small iron gate in the middle which take you up some stone stairs and into the second floor. The gate on the right was also small. When you go through it, you can either turn left or right for the bottom half of the school. If you turn right you can go right around the back

Just by the big gates was a big spreading mango tree. I saw this figure was climbing up on the wall next to the big gates. I quickly placed my bike at the side and went to check. I sent a message quickly to the station. As I got to the wall, I saw clearly who it was. It was the killer. When he saw me, he let go of the wall, turned and ran down the yard, heading towards the bay. It was a long way to go, and I was right behind him. At the bottom of the school yard was a cliff, it ended right by the tall tamarind tree where a small sandy track led down to the sandy beach, and then the rocks with the sea splashing over them.

It was dark but still clear enough to see in front of you. He got to the edge of the cliff and jumped over, landed on the soft sand, turned to his left and started running. The cliff down to the sand wasn't that high. So there was no chance of anyone hurting themselves, the rocks were too far away to be landing on them. I followed him but there was still some distance between us. I knew what he was heading for. On the left, near to the beach was a sugar cane field. It went right up to the main road. If he gets into it before I reach him, I've lost all chance of catching him. Behind me, I realize there were many policemen prodding heavily through the sand.

The killer got to the cane field before me and slipped in. It was dark in there. I still went in, breaking down the cane from their branches. Then I stopped. Listening to hear noise, there was none. Some policemen were close behind me. We stayed still for ten minutes. Still no movement.

Brown and Sampson I heard was at the front of the school and a cordon had already been set along the main road. The field opposite had already been set on fire some time ago, and the cane cutters had already cut it down. So he could get no cover from that one. Next to the cane field he was now in, there was a row of houses, and at the front, they lined the main road. There was another cane field just up on the right. What would he do? Would he cross the main road and make himself an easy target? What we didn't know was, he had already left the cane field and was at the side of one of the houses., and waiting for a good opportunity to quickly run across and be safe in that sugar cane field. This field ran the length of the main road going out of town. There was only a track between it and the other field. It was going to be very difficult for us to cover the whole area.

The killer moved up, going through the yards, and then he went back down to the bay where there was no sand--only rocks. Over the rocks were trees hanging low almost into the sea. Beneath these trees, he hid then moved out into a field well away from us.

We still had enough policemen with us to track him down. He knew the cane fields well so he could slip in and out as he wished. We were now not very far away from the road leading up to the big estate. There were four cane fields very long and with over twenty rows each. there were two on the right-hand and two on the left. The rail line ran through the middle. It had now become even darker, but we still had light from the search lights and from the street lamp posts. Soon they'll go out and the place would become even darker. That was the time he would have a chance to slip through us. I now felt that this operation is going to take us all through the night. Detective Brown too, felt that this operation would last long. If need be, he would stay around until the killer was caught. But what if he had already slipped through without us seeing him. He would be long gone, leaving us there as fools.

I was surprised when detective Brown said, "Take some men and go up along the track by the rail line. Take enough to cover that area."

I said, "What about the two sides, they're open."

He said, "I know that, but that's a chance we have to take."

While we were busy at the front and where the houses were,

the killer was moving quickly along the sea shore over the black rugged rocks. He had the thick trees hanging down and almost touching the rocks to hide him. Approximately two kilometers from the cordon off area; and on another estate. Moving up from the sea, crossed the main road quickly, all in the dark of the night, hid himself in the first rows of a small thick cane field. From where he was, he could clearly if anyone was coming. In case he saw anyone coming, he would go deeper in the field, and lie low.

From the cordon off area to where he was, the road ran up a hill and down on the other side. We could not in any way see him. The one thing we didn't want to happen has taken place. Safely now on a small estate adjacent to the big one. It hadn't got as many cane fields as the big one. Very far away it was from the main road which goes to the capital. There's a big hill in front of it known as Cathorn Hill. At the back right at the foot there were thick trees. The killer got a ride on a horse-drawn cart for one kilometer. He got off, went through a long five row cane field, down a small slope, and rested beneath a big tree. There, he stayed for about two hours. Out of sight he could not be seen. If anyone had come down towards the tree, he would have seen them and made his escape.

The killer so far had given us a run for our money. We had many more policemen to aid us. They had come from the capital. All we need now was to get back on his track.

A few tractors had come down the paved path beside Cathorn hill to take the sugar cane to the sliding just at the foot of the hill. Most of the sugar cane fields were cut down and it was going to be very hard for the killer to conceal himself in the low land. The idea came to him of moving up into the mountains and even in the thick forest. It was impossible to go hungry with so many fruit trees around, and the sugar cane was there. After thinking about it for a while, he decided it was a good thing to do. Making his way higher up, pass the small estate, he came on a very high ground. Before that, he had to cross a long bridge. At one end was thick forest, and at the other end sugar cane fields on either side. At one time he was thinking about going up on Cathorn hill. From there he could also get a good look down below and see what has happening. Where he was now, one could see for miles around, and he felt okay for the time being.

Detective Brown had a plan as well. With the policemen, we all went to the small estate. We saw there a big cage with talking birds. There was a mountain ridge just at the back of the estate. The woods, one could see were thick. A cassava field ran right up to the edge. More plantations were seen around the area. There were lots of grasshoppers around too.Getting to where the killer was would be a very hard task for the police. He had a clear view for miles around with the forest only a few feet away.

Inside this forest youths came up from the town to chop down dry wood, even green wood as well to take back and given to the bakeries for money or for bread. Three youths had come out of the forest with wood upon their heads and heading down the steep hill, and saw on their right, a man inside a half shelter shading from the sun. They kept to themselves and was glad when they were finally out of his sight. Back in town they reported what they had seen to the police station.

The forest the killer was nearby was vey big it went for miles deep within, and also in length. We had a job on our hands if he entered that forest. We had packed lunches and was driven close to the long bridge. Carefully we walked across the boarded path and got to the other side without encountering a train.

Above the small estate we came to the mountain leading

up to the forest. Detective Brown, Sampson and myself were leading the way. The track up the mountain was small. Half way up, we could see the town below, Cathorn hill just to the left, with the vast ocean staring back at us. It was still early in the morning, about 10:30 am.

I watched some policemen how they stopped now and then to catch their breath. This mountain was high, it was taking quite a lot out of us. Detective Brown had already gotten hold of some foresters, they knew the area well. Some policemen had gone on a track with one of the foresters on the right of the small estate. Three kilometers in they had come to a deep slit in the forest; walking close by; they had to take care not to slip and fall over into the great deep below. After about five kilometers it ended, and they could get around it. The plan was for them to get to the area, north, where the killer was. Leaving where he was, he started walking along the edge of the forest north-westerly. We finally got where he had been, sat down for a well-deserved rest.

Detective Brown wasn't pleased at all. There wasn't anything he could do about it. We had our plans, and so did the killer.He wasn't planning to fall into our hands just yet.

Up on this high mountain the view was spectacular, now its back down, and without the killer.

The killer made his way along the edge of the forest making sure to keep out of sight. He was now not very far away from Crystal Ridge. Plans to move down to the group of trees were in his mind. There he could rest. It was quite a safe place now. He had left the police high up on the mountain behind the small esate. Again, he knew he was safe. More plans were coming to him to find real safety. Resting he might come up with something. There's one thing he must always have in mind--the police won't ever give up--hunting him down.

He got himself safely to Crystal rydge and rested beneath the group of trees. From there he had a good view all around. His escape route was clear. As he laid back on the tree root, he started remembering what had happened that evening when his wife and himself started quarreling. He recalled that this happened almost every night when he came back from work. The Friday evening, he began to remember clearly, he had taken hold of his machete and went out to frighten her. It all got out of hand, and she ended being killed. He had panicked and made his plan to take her out to sea. After he had done so, he knew he could no longer stay around especially later, when they had found the bag with the body. From that time until now he had been on the run.

Something startled him. he got quickly onto his feet; it was only a mongoose.

The killer's brother came back from the island that was close to ours. He had been away for a few weeks. They met in one of their usual hideouts. The brother urged the killer to go away to the island, he refused. The brother explained to him that he would be safe there. The authorities weren't worried about men like us and weren't interested in giving us over to the police. They were happy with the business they were making with the smugglers. Only when they got back to our island, they found themselves in serious trouble with the special police force. The killer would have nothing of what his brother was saying. He was willing to stay and face what should come.

Detective Brown had a file with all the information about the killer's brother. But he had no information when he left and returned to the island. In fact, no one had any idea where he was at this moment.

After chatting with his brother, the killer went to his own hideout away from prying eyes.

Saturday night at the northend of the island the secret special police lay wait for a boat that was heading towards our island. The boat had left the small island, it had two occupants; these smugglers always go down in twos; nearing our island there was only one occupant. In the deep dangerous waters, an argument had cropped up between them The stronger one had overpowered the weaker one. They struggled for a while until the weaker one was battered over the head and tossed overboard in the swift flowing waters. As the boat drew nearer to the shore, the stronger man was waiting for a signal which never came. He waited for a while trying to pierce with his eyes along the shore. It was dark. He saw nothing. He came nearer to the shore. As soon as he hopped out onto the sand, the special police was there. They grabbed him, he was the killer's brother. He was the man who had freed his brother, the killer. They tried to force information from him about the whereabouts and hiding place of the killer. They got nothing from him. He was taken to the capital's prison.

We did an operation on the small estate between the town and Sorrell Ground. It was lying way down from the main road on the left near the sea. It only had a little sugar cane fields. We found notheing there.

Monday morning at the station detective Brown was looking at the map of the area. Then suddenly, he said: "Look at this!" Sampson and I drew nearer and took a look. There staring back at us was Benjamin's plantation between Crystal Ridge and Sorrell Ground. I knew the plantation was there. It was very small and private.

"Get the trucks, get the policemen, we"re going there." Detective Brown said. "Don't get too close with the trucks. Leave them half-way, walk the rest." We did as detective Brown commanded.

It took a long time walking the other half up to Benjamin's plantation. We left the track, went up to a wooden gate on our left, opened it and found ourselves on a track leading deeper into the place. On the right was a grove of mango trees, coconut trees were in between. Looking on our left we saw two small cane fields with a few rows of peanuts and cassava in the middle of them. The rows of the cane field were very short. Deeper in, we came to a wire fence, high on the left side, but very low on the right side where one could just hop over.

There behind the wire fence was a cane field which did not belong to the plantation. Farther down on the left was a sort of shed. There was a barrel with a tap filled with water There were more fruit trees at the bottom. We came back close to the wire fence where it was low on the right. I heard a slight rustle of thrash. Sampson heard it too with his back towards the fence with detective Brown just in front of him and some policemen. He probably hadn't heard anything. I was looking to see if it was some wild animal like a mongoose or a goat that had pulled up its stake and took off. This happened quite often. It was no mongoose or goat, it was a man crouching down.

I moved across the fence like a bullet, at the same time he rushed away, and was making his way through the field for the other end. the noise could be heard a long way off. Have you ever tried running through a full grown cane field? It is something that is very hard to do. At the end of the cane field was a small forest. I stood there breathing heavily looking left and right along the track. I went a few meters in the forest, but nothing. A bit further in, came to a small stream, I crossed it, then went up out of the forest, and came to the edge of another cane field. I stopped, listened, heard nothing unusual. I was on my own. The policemen and the other detectives were left way behind.

I went through this second cane field and came to an open field where women were planting potato vines. I asked one of them if they had seen a well- built man. They hadn't seen anyone. I was thinking he could be lying low in the forest, but that could be a stupid thing to do with so many policemen around. They themselves hadn't seen anyone. I was absolutely sure I had seen the figure of a man. Not long after I joined up with the two detectives and the rest of the policemen. The policemen who had cordoned off Benjamin's plantation hadn't seen anyone. I was also thinking, could he be lying low in the cane field beside the wire fence? There's only one way to find out--and that is to go in row by row. This cane field wasn't cordoned off.Policemen were between it and the fence. What I think has actually happened is that the killer must have doubled tracked when he got to the end of the field when I had been chasing him. Moving up a couple rows, it was easy to hide behind a very thick bunch of cane, with the light and dark thick thrash to hide him along with the overlapping canes. Row by row he could move up to the next cane field. That one wasn't cordoned off, so he could be safe there. We went through the field behind the fence row by row and found nothing.

Through and through we went in the field above,but he was long gone. Sampson said when we were back out on the track,"I'd like to give that guy a good thump.."

"Who wouldn't," I replied. We have to catch him first. He's very slippery!"

Detective Brown said: "We'll catch him, don't worry about that. He can give us the slip as many times as he wants, but we'll trap him.

8

Carnival Festival

IT WAS TIME for the Carnival festival. Men and women were dressed up in beautiful costumes. They were dancing and singing as they went along the street. I watched the plays and listened to some speeches. The players were wearing headdress with peacock feathers with small glasses sewn in their costumes. The wild mass started, they performed within a circle pushng back the spectators. People were dancing the jig and boillola. It is beautiful to watch how those dancers perform. The clowns came on, and the street theatre--the Bull play. The big drum assembly was next: bass drum, kettle drum and bamboo fifes. Many steel drum bands joined the ceremony. Women and men were jumping up and down like mad. Their bottoms wriggling as they dance to the music.

Detective Brown and Sampson were on the other side over against me. I saw some policemen approached him. Then he waved over to me. I made my way through the thick crowd and got to where he was. I heard the news from him. They had a new lead on the killer. He was down on a bay bathing at the shore. This was a secluded bay difficult to get to because of all the sugar cane fields that surrounded it. The surrounding cliffs on the right were jagged and high,having the cane fields on top. There was a winding path down to the bay, and to the sand that spread here and there. A split was in the cliffs with a path leading up to the cane fields. That was the killer's route to the cane fields. He had to get through it before the policemen had time to surround it. The cane fields came right to the edge of the cliff. It was easy to go through the path between the cliffs and through the cane field which was partly broken down to make a path through it.

The killer was at the edge of the sea, naked, bathing himself. From his position he could look behind and see the stalks of canes waving slightly with the cool wind. He knew if there was any trouble he could rush to the field and disappear. On his right, and at the back, the cliff was high, with a terrible winding path down to the bay. Even a fit person has to take care when coming down that path. There was also at the far end a cemented wall with a few steps leading up from the bay. This was a little out into the sea.

Meeting detective Brown and Sampson during the festival was coincidental. Detective Brown said, "Jay G, I think we have him this time. He's down at High Cliff Bay."

"What a fool," I said. "He could have just come and give himself up to us and save all the trouble."

"No, Jay G," detective Brown said, "it's not that easy. He has picked a spot that is rather difficult for us. We have to plan this carefully, if we want to take him in."

Sampson said: "What we are planning to do is not to frighten him away. We will make him think that he is safe where he is, by not rushing in too quickly. We shall cordon off the cane fields directly behind him. There's no other way down but by that winding dangerous path; and the steps on the right, and through the cliffs."

"What about along the bay to his left or right?" I asked

Detective Brown said, "The bay goes round in a half circle with heavy rocks along it up to the cliff. The sea is always lashing hard in that place."

"It still sounds a bit tricky to me." I made my point clear.

"Jay G," detective Brown said, "You and Sampson with

policemen will come from his left down that dangerous path. Be careful. I'll take the rest and make our way to the right of him."

Washing himself quickly, the killer clothed himself and rushed through the cliff, taking the path of the broken down canes. The detectives knew about the path through the cliffs but didn't know about the broken down canes making a path through the field. That was done by the natives making a short cut to the bay. As he went through the cliffs he immediately took a track that led up onto the cliffs where the end of the cane field terminated. He planned to edge his way along. This part of the field could not be cordoned off, it was too close to the edge of the cliff. It could be done if they stay a few meters in.

Jay G knew about this area, and he too, carefully started edging his way along hanging on to the thick canes as he moved. He left Sampson and the policemen back there at the path going down to the bay. Jay G had a whistle and if he needed help he could always blow it. But he rarely ever did so.

The killer stopped behind a great bunch of sugar canes, he crouched low. About six bunches away, Jay G stopped, listening for sounds, he heard none. He moved cautiously to his left and now was about two bunches from where the killer was, crouching on the left side of a bunch of canes. As soon as Jay G moved to slide himself across to where the killer was, not knowing he was there, the killer rose up and lashed out at Jay G. Both men had to be careful. One slip and they would go over the cliff. below was sand and stones. Jay G hangs on to some sugar canes with his right hand hugging himself into the bunch and at the same time trying to use his left to try and get hold of the killer.

Jay G took the chance by letting go of his right, steadying

himself and as soon as the killer came at him again, Jay G did a quick rugby tackle taking the killer with him a few centimeters away from the cliff. The killer had both arms around Jay G's neck as they both lay there at the root of a bunch of canes. The killer got on his knees, then on his feet still with Jay G's head fast in a lock; moving slowly inwards, dragging Jay G as he went along. Jay G was trying all the while to wriggle his head out the grip, but the killer was strong, he was a fighter, he couldn't be easily overpowered by one or even two people.

Suddenly, Jay G got his feet between the killer's and began kicking like a horse. The killer eased his grip and the head of Jay G came free. He began using his head as a ramming rod. The killer held on tight, dragging Jay G to the ground. With his right hand the killer tried to bring a lethal right across the face of Jay G.

Jay G twisted his head, held on tightly to the killer, up on his feet Jay G tossed him away, the killer came back lashing out with a right into the wind. Jay G gave him a good left into the stomach, the killer went down, reaching out to grab one of the legs of Jay G, he failed to do so. Jay G gave him a kick in the right side, the killer curled up in pain. Jay G picked him up, holding one hand tugged him into his right knee which he brought up for that sole purpose. That did the trick, the killer fell in pain, and failed to rise up.

Detective Brown and his policemen came on the scene, they had come in from the left and made their way up to where we were. Sampson and the policemen who were waiting at the track leading down to the bay knew nothing of what was going on between Jay G and the killer. They took him away. Detective Brown said, "Great work, Jay G."

Sampson came and said, "Well done, Jay G."

I said, "Our team has done a great job, thanks!"

A few days after the capture of the killer I got invited to a wedding. One of the men in my old group from the big estate was getting married. At the wedding, I met that overseer. He surprised me, by coming over and saying, "I heard of the capture of that killer! Your team has done a good job."

I said, "Thanks, and by the way, no hard feelings."

9

Jay G goes to England

THE BIG SHIP was in the harbour schedule to sail in 3 hours time to England. There were many people on the dockside saying their last goodbyes. Jay G was smartly dressed as he boarded the ship. He had never been on a ship like this before, this was all new to him.

My cabin was down below, and was lucky to have one of the ship's steward to help with my luggage. We finally got to my cabin, and he opened the door. On my left, in the same cabin was a young woman about 18 years old. I said, "Sorry! Wrong cabin," and turned to leave. The steward said that this was the right cabin and continued taking my luggage in. What a situation this was? I've never known anything like this before. I finally took it all in, and settled down to this strange arrangement.

I began to get the feeling after I had settled in, that something wasn't right. Whatever it was, I said to myself, I'll play along. I also saw that the girl didn't mind that she had to share a cabin with me, for two whole weeks. "Do you mind if I ask you where you're from?

"Not at all," she looked at me very friendly. "My name is Sarah, and I'm from Crayon."

"I know the place. Been through it a few times. I'm from the Point, next to Sorrell Ground."

"Nice place, nice people!"

"Thank you!" I said. "Are you alone on the ship? Or maybe you have others with you?"

"I'm alone," she told me.

"Have you got family?" I asked.

"My mother and father passed away after being in a car accident. I have a few aunts and uncles around."

"Sorry to hear that. It is sad losing both parents like that."

"Yes, I know. It is the way of life, and we just have to accept it."

"That's true," I told her.

As the days slipped by Sarah and I got friendlier, went to the restaurant, and the swimming pool together. We did almost everything together, except going to bed. There were no feelings between us for that sort of thing. She knew my name to be Jay G; but knew nothing about me being a constable. I concealed that part away from her, but we did discuss over the murder case that was going on at my place. "So they finally caught the killer, and put him away," she said. to me.

"Rightly so," I said. He gave them a hard time, but in the long run, they nabbed him. Tell me, what are you going to do when you get to England?"

"I've trained to be a nurse, and when I get there, I'll be meeting up with my boyfriend."

"Now it makes sense to me."

"What makes sense to you?" She asked with a smile on her face.

"The nurse and the boyfriend part. And I'm glad that I didn't approach you."

"I would have screamed and all the stewards would have come rushing in, and carried you away."

"Really? I had no intention of doing anything anyway!"

"And what if I had approached you? What would you have done?"

"That would have been a terrible situation for me." I replied.

"It's rather hard now to say what I would have done. You're a very attractive young girl, and I would have been thinking that there must be something wrong."

"On a ship, way out in the ocean? What could have been wrong?"

"Well, you never know. Anyway, it didn't turn out like that."

"I'm a nurse and well-trained to deal with such situations. Dealing with people, we are kind, compassionate, and friendly. We know how to avoid strange situations." Sarah said.

I left Sarah in the cabin and went out for an early morning walk, just before breakfast. The sea was calm, and the boat moved along steadily. From my deck, I went up a few steps to the next deck, and it was there that I met trouble. There weren"t many people around, only a few here and there.. On this deck there were hardly anyone around. I walked along it, looking over in the sea below, then I felt a nudge. I turned my head slightly, and saw out the corner of my eye, two blokes, standing there. They were big like wrestlers. I turned around and saw their faces. No friendly look at all. Only the three of us were on this deck. I quickly looked to the right, and saw the stairs leading up, and to my left, those leading down. With speed, I moved away from them, and ran to the stairs leading up. They were too slow to try and stop me. On the deck above, I made for the steps leading higher up. I finally got to where the funnels were--big massive things with smoke coming out. I placed myself in a position where I could easily see when someone approached.

Before those two brutes came close to me again, I had been thinking fast what to do. There beside me on the ground was a roll of thick ropes. Maybe I could use that to get myself over the deck barrier, and down to the lower decks. At this time in the morning, most people were still in bed, so no help would come from that area. Many things were going through my head Why all of a sudden, these two guys just turn up? Who were they? And what were they after? I can't recall being in any trouble except being a constable helping the detectives on that murder case. No. I said, 'It can't have anything to do with that.' Just then, the two blokes came into my view. They were now a few meters away from me. I stepped out bravely, confronting them. "What the hell do you want?" No sooner had I said that when I received a fist in my guts. It hurt, but I grabbed one of the guys around his neck. He was struggling to free himself, I just wouldn't let go. I could break his neck if I wanted to. My instructor back at the police station had taught me quite a few things. The other guy backed off.. I let go of the guy I was holding when I saw two stewards coming our way. I walked away and went down the stairs leading to the deck below. If the stewards hadn't come our way, I'm quite sure the ship's hospital bed would have been available for one of the three of us. Up against an enemy, I never give up no matter what. I defend myself as good as I can.

Getting back to my cabin, Sarah saw that there was something wrong. My face had that angry look. I had to explain to her what had taken place. She was trying to figure out why they want to attack me, and could not explain why. "Breakfast is coming up, are you in the mood for it?" She asked me.

"Sure!" I said.

Breakfast didn't go down well. I was too choked up about what had happened. "I see you've no appetite today." Sarah told me.

"I just can't swallow anything down at the moment."

"Are you injured? Did they hurt you?"

"No. I only took a punch in the belly from one of them," I said. "I'm okay. Nothing to worry about."

The following day I managed to get my breakfast down, my lunch, and also the dinner. It turned out be a good day. Sarah and I went all around the boat meeting up with different people, and chatting. The boat had already called in to a few places on the way up, and the trip started to become enjoyable. We stayed on board, and didn't go in the small boats to visit the islands. The next stop was St Vincent, and the boat came right in. We came down many steps and down to the wharf platform. There were many shops, and at the back and sides, some beautiful painted houses. It was like in a dream. This was no dream, this was real. A taxi came but we did not take it. Instead, we walked some distance away from the boat, looking at the beautiful gardens, trees, and houses. Night was falling and the whole boat was lit up like in a circus. So beautiful this was. We got back onto the boat, and back in our cabin. The boat pulled away from St. Vincent, and went along its way for the next stop. "Tell me something about your boyfriend," I said to Sarah. "Where is he staying?"

"He went up from Crayon, got himself a job in Nottingham main hospital. It took him quite some time to save up some money, and then he sent for me to come over."

"And you too, is going to work at the same hospital?"

"Yes, I'm afraid so."

"Nottingham is the place where I'm heading for. I hope that I'm lucky and get myself a reasonable job that pays well. I will try the police and see if I could get to do what I was doing back home."

"That would be good if it works out that way for you." Sarah told me.

"It would be just great if I could do the same work."

"My boyfriend wrote that the police in Nottingham is very busy trying to clean up the place because there are so many people committing crimes. I think that you'll have a lot on your hands when you get there."

"I'm prepared to take on whatever comes along." I told Sarah.

"It's not like back on our island. In England most of the places have crimes to do with guns and knives, and stealing and murders. The policemen have to defend themselves, so they carry weapons."

"That means that I too, if I get a job with the police, I'll be carrying a gun?"

"That's just the way it is, and it has been like that for a very long time now. Sarah explained.

Our boat was doing at least 180 kilometres per day. At that rate, it would be on time in Southampton. So far, the weather stayed beautiful, clear skies, beautiful islands, clear views of everything. We got to Venezuela, and had a good time there. For days we saw only seas, the blue skies, and now and then a cruise ship.

One day late in the afternoon, just gone past lunch, Sarah and I were both out by the swimming pool. This was situated on the middle deck, at the front part of the boat. There were only two free deck chairs left, and believe it or not, the two thugs were on the left of them, lazing back in their deck chairs. They both squinted up at us, using their hands to protect their eyes from the blaring sunlight. The taller of the two said, "Look who we have here?"

I said to him, "You're asking for a thick lip, and from me, you'll get it!"

They started laughing.

"If you get too much on my nerves, I'll just go and make a report of you to the captain. He will soon sort both of you out.. Tell me, what do you want from me?"

Sarah stretched herself out on one of the chairs while I carried on talking to the blokes.

"You've no protection here now," the shortest one told me. "There are no police and detectives here to protect you."

"Just to let you know, you ignorant fools, there are security people on this boat, and there is also a cell, where they can put you away, should you do something foolishly."

"Like you put our friend away, you'd like to do the same to us?" The tallest one spoke.

"Don't you know that he committed a murder and deserves to be where he is now? It shows what type of people you are."

In the swimming pool area, there were many people bathing in the sun. Waiters were busy with drinks of all sort. Some people were listening to our conversation for they weren't far away. "We are still going to get you for what you have done," the short one let me know.

"For me, justice is done, and I'm not going to lose any sleep over it. You had better watch yourselves, for I would get you arrested as soon as we get to Southampton. Don't push your luck with me?" I left them and went to the empty deck chair besides Sarah.

She said, "I see that you have told them off, you have done the right thing. They have to be careful while on the ship."

"I wouldn't worry about them any more."

10

Arrival in Nottingham

THE SHIP CAME in to dock on time. Passengers started getting off. Sarah and I made our way to the train station, and took a train that would take us to Birmingham and then to Nottingham. The journey would be about 4 hours and some minutes. On our island we have about 18 miles of train through beautiful scenery. Here in England you can spend hours on the train before you get to where you want to go. We saw quite a lot on the way up to Nottingham. In Birmingham we changed trains, and finally got to the Midland Station in Nottingham. The station was big and I learned later that there was an old station called Victoria, In 1904 trains started running from the Midland Station. We got off the train, Sarah and I, walked up a few steps then came to the over deck car park. There, Neil was waiting for Sarah. He was a nice friendly chap, we chatted for a bit, I said so long to Sarah, giving her my phone number and address. Taking a taxi, we then parted.

The traffic on the main road was heavy, but we got to the place where I was to stay just under fifteen minutes. I paid the taxi, took my luggage inside, and found my room. I had a shower and a quick meal and went out to the English pub. While I was back home, news came to me about these pubs, so now I could experience it myself.

I got into conversation straight away, and the drinks kept coming in. I had to tell all about my homeland, and what the people there were like. I must confess, this pub business was really great. The places were packed on the day when Nottingham Forest were playing at home. And yes, I got to see my first footbal match.

I stepped out the pub a bit tipsy, and started making my way to the place where I stay. Suddenly, as I turned up this lane flanked by walls, this youth of about twenty came at me. I saw the flash of the knife in his hand, and moved quickly to divert his attack. Lights were shining at the far end of this lane, for it wasn't that long. I became sober immediately and tried to wrestle with this youth. He was a strong one and managed to get the knife near my ribs. I felt the tip of it against them. "Give me your wallet," he said, "or you get it."

I said to him, "I don't carry any wallet around with me. I only have a few changes."

"That will do," he took what I gave him and ran away.

Luck was with me this night, I came out of the lane unscathed. The youth believed what I had told him. Searching me he would have found that I had a wallet in my inside pocket loaded with pound notes. Finding my way, I got back to where I was staying. Tomorrow I had to go up to the town for an interview at the police station. I wanted to see if it was possible to work with the police.. I got all the information I needed from the interview. The possibility of being a detective was good. Interviewing witnesses and getting down to what is true was very important in the community. Because I only just came to the country, I must wait for three years, then take some exams, and complete a two-year programme. There was no problem there, I was still young and wasn't in a big hurry.

I was having fun hopping on and off the Double Decker buses. At the back, below, the conductor would stand while he checked and hand out tickets, and collecting the money. He would also go through the bus checking on the new arrivals.

Sometimes the bus driver would speed away leaving you running like mad to try and hop on.

Overall I found the place rather safe except for a few crazy kids who went now and then on a rampage with their knives. One night coming back from the town, and being at the top of the bus, a few kids were messing about. It became too much for me, so I turned around and said, "Will you cool it down?" I should have known, I just stirred up a viper's nest. From the back, they came to where I sat, just in the middle on the right-hand side. "Are you talking to us," one of them said. "Let's hope you're not for you'll regret it!"

I didn't wait for I saw what they were going to do. I grabbed the one nearest to me and shuffled quickly to the steps leading down, and gave him a push.

The others came at me, at the same time the bus came to a halt. The knives came out, and the conductor was already on the stairs coming up, and me making my way down at the same time. I got off the bus and took a taxi home.

I had no intention waiting around to be stabbed up by these young kids. They will see more of me when I finally get to work with the police. For now, I'll just try to keep away from trouble and concentrate on getting the job with the police.

The years flew by and I finally got to do my police training which took about 6 months, then after a few years of hard work and exams, I got to be a detective. I was already a constable in my own country working with detectives, but here in England it was different. They had different rules.

The occasion came where I had to work with the police and sniffer dogs. Such a thing was not known back home. I've been on a few cases, but the one which turned out to be rather interesting, was the one at Bulwell. Bulwell was just outside Nottingham, about 7 kilometres away. My team and I got there to investigate a criminal case. We were attacked violently by some males, and I ended up in the Nottingham hospital with face injuries.

Sarah came into the ward, came to my bed, and draw the curtain around it. "Hello there again," she said. "See you got yourself into trouble?"

I tried to smile, that was impossible, with the bandages still on my face. "Hello," I said. "The work I do is trouble. Glad to see you again!"

"I'll just take off these bandages on your face, and dress it with new ones. As soon as she was finished with the dressing, we began to talk about how it was going with my work, and also hers. I told her all about my training and being now a full detective She told me that she was happy here as a nurse. "I have had many people in here from that place where you got your injuries. It has a very bad record," Sarah said to me. "In one years time there were more than 40, 000 crime offences."

"The people there just don't seem to care. They ignore the police dogs," I said.

Sarah said to me, "Your face should be well in a few months time. I don't think there'll be any scars to be seen. Luck was really with you!"

"But I know in our work this sort of thing is to be expected."

"Didn't you have your guns on you?" Sarah asked.

"Only special units get to carry them," I told her. "Many people got arrested.

Sarah then told me the good news. "Neil and I are going to be married"

I said, "That's great news, Sarah, congratulations."

"In two months time it will happen. You'll get the invitation soon."

"I saw when I first met Neil at the rail station that both of you would make a good pair." I told her.

After she was satisfied that the dressing was okay, she went away.

Three months after going to Sarah's wedding, I found myself investigating a kidnapping case. A young child had been taken from its pram outside a small drugstore. The team and I got cracking interviewing as many people as we could who had probably seen or heard something to do with the case. Some one had seen a man wrapped in heavy cloak passed by the drug store. He kept looking around all the time, suspiciously. A few people passed by as well, it was just coming up for nine in the morning.

We had nothing solid to go on, many witnesses say that they had seen this, others, they had seen that, but it all came down to nothing. Then we got a lead onto the man who was seen that morning wearing the heavy cloak. The mother of the kidnapped child said she had left the child in the pram, by the door, and had quickly nipped in to buy something. Coming back out, she found the pram empty. More investigations brought us back to Bulwell. We were much more prepared this time. It was like walking into a snake's nest, you don't know exactly what's going to happen. Sometimes they use violence and sometimes they dont. The main thing was, to make sure that you had a few police vans ready in case trouble brew up. In our job, that sort of thing happen often. For although we knew that this place had a very high percentage of violence, no policeman was scared at all to go there. They went there as if it was a normal peaceful place, which it wasn't.

We entered into the street where we were told the man in the heavy cloak lived. There was already a crowd gathering, all nosy so-and so's. This big stropping bloke came over. "Who are you looking for?" He asked.

I said, "It's not you we are looking for, so you can relax."

He grinned and said, "Funny cop!"

We went up to the door of the address that we were given, and pushed the door bell. I saw someone peeped from behind the curtain, then the door was open. The door was opened wider and he let us in. We asked him a few questions. He admitted that he was the man around at the time, by the small drugstore. We listened as he began to confess that he had taken the child from its pram; but this was done for a woman who lived a couple streets away. Noting down the address, we took the man away with us to the other address. There, we spoke with the woman who had been given the child. Inside the house, we found the child fast asleep in a cot.

Both the man and the woman were arrested; and the baby was taken back to its rightful parents. More investigations were held to do with other cases; and they were really piling up. On a week end off I went to see Nottingham Forest play. I visited the pub,had a chat and a drink, then left. Back at work the following week, we found ourselves in Beeston. Beeston is about 5 kilometres from Nottingham. This case had to do with a young boy who had been hit by a car. The car didn't stop. Someone had noted the number of the vehicle. One witness, a woman, told us that she was standing beside a tree on the opposite side of the road, and had seen clearly what had happened.

The car had come along, hit the boy who was walking along at the side of the road, and sped away. The boy was then taken to the hospital where he died. We worked on this case for a whole year. An address came up from the car registration office. Arriving at the address, there was no one living there. The car was found in an old scrap yard. The driver, a young man, was drinking in a bar, when we went in and arrested him. After this case had come to a close, I was staying with some friends nearby to the Nottingham Forest football grounds. The evening kick-off was due around 20:45. I was the only one who had a great interest in football, so I left my friends , and started walking towards the stadium.

Not far away was a grove of medium trees, very bushy. As I came walking by, two blokes stepped out and grabbed me, tucking me under cover into the grove. They were the blokes from the ship--the tall and short one. I struggled hard to free myself, but they had me fast. I said to them, "This is foolish you know. I only have to yell, and in no time at all, people walking along would come and check. They gagged me, in the darkness, took me to a nearby car. I knew the area pretty well, and as the car started up and drove away, I began mentally to keep a check of where it was driving to. There was an old broken down ware house by the Trent, and that's where they pulled in to. Even with the gag on, and hands tied, I was thinking If I had a chance to escape from these two thugs. Shall I risk it? Then as they came around to my door, and tried to get me out, I started grabbing and tugging. I had a head inside the back seat, while the feet were still outside on the ground. The car was rocking like mad as I held on to one of them and won't let go. They had tied my hands at the front, foolish that was, I still had enough space to maneuver, using my arms and elbows, I gathered up all my strength, and held on courageously.

The other guy, the tall one, went to the other door, opened it, and gave me an enormous whack. I let the guy I hand between my elbows go, and fell back on the leather seat.

I came to, feeling the pain coming from my head. There was a big bump, there was no blood. I was at the side of the Trent. Luckily, they had not thrown me in. I started feeling around for my mobile, it was gone. I had only enough money on me to get my ticket, and a few drinks, that too was gone. I didn't have a gun on me, only special firearms people, and secret service are allowed to have that. Also, policemen in an emergency would sometimes carry firearms.

I was spotted by a few early fishers who had come down to cast their line in the Trent. They came over and asked if everything was alright. I told them, yes, I'm okay. Holding my head, I made my way back to where my friends live. I told them all about what had happened and how I met those blokes on the way up on the ship. Landing at Southampton, and Sarah and I, how we caught the train to Nottingham. I thought that was it, I'll never see those blokes again. I was wrong. I heard too, that Forest had won the match. Just my luck not to be there. The swelling on my head started going down, and I was lucky there wasn't much damage. I got back into the swing of my work again, and started enjoying it more and more. Sarah and her husband visited me a few times. Two years later, I was walking down the isle, getting married, and about to start my own family.

The End.